DANGER ON ICE

Lisa Wroble

STECK-VAUGHN
ELEMENTARY · SECONDARY · ADULT · LIBRARY

A Harcourt Company

www.steck-vaughn.com

Photography: Cover ©Hulton Archives/Getty Images;
p.iii ©Scott Polar Research Institute; pp.iv-1 ©Jan Tove
Johanssons/Getty Images; p.3 ©Scott Polar Research Institute;
p.5 ©Hulton Archives/Getty Images; p.6 ©Barry Rosenthal/Getty
Images; p.9 ©Scott Polar Research Institute; p.11 ©Scott Polar
Research Institute; p.12 ©Scott Polar Research Institute; p.13
©Scott Polar Research Institute; p.15 ©Hulton Archives/Getty
Images; p.17 ©Scott Polar Research Institute; p.18 ©Scott Polar
Research Institute; p.19 ©Jan Tove Johanssons/Getty Images;
p.20 ©Scott Polar Research Institute; pp.22–23 ©Scott Polar
Research Institute.

Additional photography by the Steck-Vaughn Collection.

ISBN 0-7398-5068-7

Copyright © 2003 Steck-Vaughn Company

Power Up! Building Reading Strength is a trademark of
Steck-Vaughn Company.

Printed in the United States of America.

5 6 7 8 9 LB 06 05 04 03

Contents

SOUTH
AMERICA

CAPE HORN

*South
Georgia
Island*

1 *Endurance* leaves
South Georgia
Island

*South Sandwich
Islands*

SOUTH
ATLANTIC
OCEAN

Elephant Island 7

6 Patience camp

5 Ocean camp

4 *Endurance* sinks

ANTARCTIC CIRCLE

2 *Endurance* hits
pack ice

SOLID
PACK
ICE

LOOSE PACK
ICE

ANTARCTIC
PENINSULA

Endurance gets
trapped in
pack ice

3

ANTARCTICA

0   200   400 miles

South
Pole ✕

SHACKLETON'S JOURNEY
TO THE SOUTH POLE

Chapter One

A Trip
to the Bottom
of the World

Today, we **explore** space. A hundred years ago, we were still exploring new land on Earth. The South Pole had just been reached. This land was new to all people. No one had ever lived at the South Pole. No one had even gone there. It was too windy. Winds of up to 200 miles an hour blew across it. It was too cold. Ice covered the land. In some places the ice was two miles deep.

Few people wanted to go to the South Pole, but many people wanted to know about it. They sent people to explore it for them.

This is the amazing story of Sir Ernest Shackleton's third trip to the South Pole.

Another Trip

It was 1914, and Sir Ernest Shackleton was ready for another trip. Shackleton was an English **explorer.** He had been to the South Pole two times before, but he had not reached the point that is the real South Pole. He had to turn back because of bad weather. In 1912, another team was the first ever to reach the South Pole. Shackleton wanted to be first to cross it.

The land at the South Pole is called Antarctica. It is a **continent** covered by ice that is four to six feet deep in most places. The trip would be long and hard, but Shackleton was ready to go again.

Paying for the Trip

The trip to Antarctica would cost a lot of money. Shackleton knew some important people. He was well known because of his other trips. Many people agreed to help pay for the trip.

Sir Ernest Shackleton led the
trip to the South Pole.

Shackleton also planned to make money.
During the trip, his team would take pictures.
The men would write in **journals**. Shackleton
would sell the story of the trip when he
returned.

Making Travel Plans

Shackleton began planning his trip. His
ship would travel south from England, then
his team would walk across Antarctica.

A second ship would sail south from Australia to Antarctica. This ship would pick up Shackleton's men and return them to England.

Getting Ready

Shackleton had a few months to get ready. First, he bought two strong wooden ships. He named one ship *Endurance. Endurance* is the strength to keep going when things are hard. This was the ship that Shackleton and his team would use to get to Antarctica. The second ship, *Aurora,* would bring them home.

Next, Shackleton needed to choose a good **crew.** The men of the *Endurance* had to be strong. They would have to live through storms with ice, snow, and wind. They would see huge **icebergs** that could break a ship to pieces. They could fall through ice into the water. Under the ice, **killer whales** swam. The killer whales ate **seals.** From under the ice, a man would look like a seal.

Shackleton and his crew get the *Endurance* ready for the long trip.

Shackleton was so well known that 5,000 people wanted to join his crew. Shackleton knew that he had to choose carefully. The right crew could mean the **difference** between life and death.

First, Shackleton chose men he knew from his other trips. Frank Wild would be second in charge. Tom Crean would be second officer. Frank Worsley would be the captain.

Next, Shackleton chose artists. The artists would draw, paint, and take pictures of Antarctica.

Then, Shackleton found a cook, doctors, and some scientists. The scientists would study the ice and the shape of Antarctica. They would also study the animals and weather.

Finally, Shackleton chose the rest of the crew. These men had sailed cold waters before.

Packing the Ship

After the crew was hired, they bought **supplies.** The men bought tents and bedding. They bought lamps and matches to light them. For food, they got canned meat and vegetables. They brought along a strange bar made of meat, vegetables, and fat. When water was added, it made soup. They bought coal to run the ship. They got tools and maps to help find their way. Shackleton bought enough supplies for two years. He knew that it was best to be safe.

Chapter Two

The Trip Begins

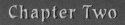

People came from far and wide to watch the crew get the ship ready for the trip. On August 8, 1914, the *Endurance* was ready to go. Everyone wished them a safe **voyage.**

After two months, the ship landed in South America. The crew rested a few weeks, then left on October 26. Three days later, they found a **stowaway.** One of the crew had helped him hide on the ship. It was too late to take the man back to land. Shackleton was angry, but he sent young Percy Blackborrow to help the cook.

Bad News

On November 5, the crew landed on South Georgia Island. **Sailors** on the island told Shackleton's men that the ice in Antarctica was very **thick.** When winter came in June, the ice would become thicker. The crew must reach Antarctica before then. They were in a race against time. The **adventure** had begun.

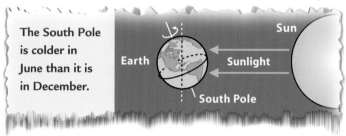

The South Pole is colder in June than it is in December.

Sun

Earth

Sunlight

South Pole

In December, the *Endurance* left South Georgia Island for Antarctica. All month the ship pushed through pack ice. This ice floated in the sea around Antarctica.

Moving through pack ice was **difficult.** The crew searched for paths. Often the ship got stuck. Then the crew jumped off the ship and broke up the ice with tools. The men were careful not to fall into ice cracks. One wrong step could be a man's last.

The crew breaks up pack ice around the *Endurance.*

Frozen in Place

On January 19, 1915, the ship stopped. This time it wouldn't move. The crew was worried. They all remembered what had happened to the *Titanic* in 1912. If a floating iceberg hit the ship, the ship might sink. The crew knew that a path might not open until spring. And spring in Antarctica was eight months away!

Chapter Three

Deeper Trouble

Six months later, the ship was still stuck. In July, the weather got worse. A **blizzard** hit. It lasted for two days. After the storm, fresh ice blocks packed tightly all around the ship.

A month later, the tightly packed ice started breaking up. But the breaking ice didn't free the *Endurance.* Instead the ice pressed against the ship. For three months, the ship made strange noises. Then on October 18, the ship suddenly lifted and fell on its side. Men and supplies flew everywhere.

At the end of October, the *Endurance* began to break into pieces. Water filled holes in the ship. The crew tried to **bail** it out, but the water kept coming in. Soon the ship would start to sink. The crew pulled supplies and three **lifeboats** off the ship.

On October 27, the men slept on ice for the first time. There were only 18 sleeping bags for 28 men. The rest of the crew used blankets. Sometimes the ice was so thin that the men felt killer whales swimming under them.

On October 18, 1915, the *Endurance* fell on its side.

Shackleton knew now that his crew would not reach the South Pole. They would not travel across Antarctica. He decided that they would go to Paulet Island. A few years before, another group had left supplies there. Paulet Island was 346 miles away, but the crew had to go. After ten months, they had used up almost half of their supplies.

The men pulled a lifeboat across the ice.

On October 30, 1915, the crew set off. They took turns pulling lifeboats filled with supplies. The boats were so heavy that it took 15 men to pull each one!

Ocean Camp

A few days later, Shackleton gave up reaching Paulet Island. They had walked less than two miles from the ship's **wreck.**

The crew set up camp on a piece of pack ice. They named it Ocean Camp.

In Ocean Camp, the crew worked hard to **survive.** They only had food for three more months, so they hunted birds and seals. The men also melted ice for drinking water.

After so much time together, some men were not getting along. All 28 men had to share five tents. Shackleton shared his tent with men he knew wouldn't get along well with the others. He knew if one man acted badly, it could be a big problem for the whole crew.

For one month, the *Endurance* slowly broke up and sank into the ocean.

The Ship Finally Sinks

Back at the wreck, the ship slipped deeper underwater. On November 21, 1915, the *Endurance* finally sank. The crew watched sadly from the camp, but Shackleton didn't let his crew lose hope. There wasn't time. The ice at Ocean Camp had started breaking up. Soon it would not be safe. It was time to leave.

Chapter Four

Moving Again

Again, Shackleton planned to reach Paulet Island. He left one lifeboat at Ocean Camp to make the **journey** easier. Pulling two heavy lifeboats would be enough work. After a few days, the crew had only gone seven miles. They hit walls of ice. With every step, the men's boots filled with ice-cold water.

For the second time, Shackleton gave up getting to Paulet Island. The crew set up a new camp. They had faced their problems with **patience.** So they called their new camp Patience Camp.

But having patience was hard. Life kept getting worse. During the day, the sun melted the ice. The crew's clothes and bedding got wet. At night, everything **froze.**

The food supply also was getting lower. The men faced great **danger** when they hunted. On January 1, 1916, Frank Wild heard a man scream. Wild saw the man being chased by a 12-foot seal. If the seal caught the man, it would **drown** him in the ocean and eat him. Quickly, Wild had to shoot the seal.

By March 1916, the crew had been **stranded** for more than a year. The men didn't think that they would ever get home again.

The Ice Begins to Melt

In March, the men felt waves moving under the ice. The ice was melting. Soon it would crack. The crew packed the lifeboats and waited for the ice to open.

The crew is getting ready to leave camp.

By late March, the ice was breaking up. Icebergs began crashing into the pack ice near Patience Camp. One huge iceberg headed toward them. At the last moment, it turned away. The men were still alive, for now.

Leaving Patience Camp

By April 8, ice was cracking all around Patience Camp. All 28 men jumped into the two lifeboats and set out for the open ocean. Killer whales circled the boats.

That night, the crew camped on an ice block. Suddenly, the ice cracked apart under a tent. One man yelled, "Somebody's missing!" Shackleton saw a sleeping bag in the water. Ernest Holness was inside! Shackleton pulled Holness from the water. The men walked Holness back and forth to keep him warm. There were no dry clothes for him. Shackleton was stuck on the other chunk of ice. The men used a lifeboat to bring him back.

Shackleton and the cook fix dinner at Patience Camp.

The next day, the crew entered the open ocean. The boats were too heavy, and they began to sink. The men returned to the ice. They had to make the lifeboats lighter. To use supplies, the crew cooked a huge meal. It was the best meal that they had eaten in months.

Escaping the Ice

As the men slept, huge waves crashed against the ice. On April 11, the men awoke to find that they were trapped. Pack ice had closed in their camp. Their ice block was breaking apart. If they didn't sail soon, they would drown.

The men watched all morning. Finally, they saw an opening in the ice pack. The crew threw their supplies in the boats, jumped in, and headed again for the open ocean.

Shackleton and his crew look tired in this picture taken in April of 1916.

Chapter Five

Endurance to the End

The men sailed for almost a week. They had no water to drink. They had **raw** seal meat to eat. Their clothes froze to their bodies. Water came into the boats, and they bailed it out. Many men got **frostbite.** Then one morning, straight ahead, they saw land.

At last, the long trip was over. They had made it to Elephant Island. For the first time in 16 months, the men walked on land. Many cried and laughed as they touched the ground.

The crew set up camp and rested. Elephant Island was covered in water. The cold wind blew ice around. The men didn't mind. They were glad to be on land.

Shackleton knew that he must get help soon or his men would die. He decided to sail back to South Georgia Island. Worsley, Crean, and three others went with him. The small crew left Elephant Island on April 24, 1916. They didn't know if they would ever see their friends again.

Shackleton and some of his crew leave Elephant Island and head for South Georgia Island.

The voyage to South Georgia Island was difficult. High waves came into the lifeboat, and the water froze. The men had to break the ice or the boat would sink. Their skin cracked and froze. Strong waves nearly crushed them against rocks. Two of the men got very sick.

After two weeks, the men landed. They rested from their trip. Then one man stayed with the two sick men while Shackleton, Worsley, and Crean went for help.

For a day and a half, the three men marched over mountains and across ice and snow. They walked 29 miles across the island. On May 20, they found the shipping **port.**

Shackleton and his men were dirty. Their clothes were torn and hanging from their bodies. Two boys at the port saw them and ran off in fear.

Sailors at the port were surprised to see the men alive. They told Shackleton that his second ship, the *Aurora,* had never left Australia.

Then the sailors sent news to England. The *Endurance* had sunk, but its crew was alive! In England and around the world, newspapers read, "Sir Ernest Shackleton Is Safe!"

On August 30, 1916, Shackleton **rescued** his 22 other men from Elephant Island. After four months, they were all still alive. When the crew reached England, they got a warm welcome home.

The crew waves as Shackleton comes to take them home.

Endurance

Shackleton and his crew never did cross Antarctica, but all 28 men had **endured.** They faced danger bravely and worked together to stay alive. Shackleton did not let his men give up, even through hard times. He gave them **courage** to face their fears and go on. Shackleton and his crew didn't win the race to cross Antarctica. But they are remembered because they faced many **risks** and survived.

Glossary

adventure (ad VEHN chuhr) *noun* An adventure is a thrilling trip or happening.

bail (BAYL) *verb* To bail means to take water out of a boat.

blizzard (BLIHZ uhrd) *noun* A blizzard is a windy, snowy storm.

continent (KAHNT ihn uhnt) *noun* A continent is a very large piece of land on Earth.

courage (KUR ihj) *noun* To have courage means to face danger bravely.

crew (KROO) *noun* A crew is the people who work on a ship.

danger (DAYN juhr) *noun* Danger is something that can hurt or kill you.

difference (DIHF uhr uhns) *noun* Difference is the way in which things are not alike.

difficult (DIHF ih kuhlt) *adjective* Difficult means hard to do.

drown (DROWN) *verb* To drown a living thing is to hold it under water until it dies.

endured (ehn DURD) *verb* To have endured means to have lasted through a hard time.

explore (ehk SPLAWR) *verb* To explore is to travel to and learn about new lands.

explorer (ehk SPLAWR uhr) *noun* An explorer is a person who travels to and learns about new lands.

frostbite (FRAWST byt) *noun* Frostbite is the harm that happens when part of the body has been touched by snow or ice.

froze (FROHZ) *verb* Froze means turned to ice or became covered in ice.

icebergs (YS burgz) *noun* Icebergs are huge chunks of ice that float in cold seas.

journals (JUR nuhlz) *noun* Journals are blank books that people write their thoughts in.

journey (JUR nee) *noun* A journey is a trip.

killer whales (KIHL uhr WAYLZ) *noun* Killer whales are very large, mostly black dolphins. They eat large fish, seals, and whales.

lifeboats (LYF bohts) *noun* Lifeboats are small boats that people use if their ship sinks.

patience (PAY shuhns) *noun* Having patience means staying calm and waiting for something without getting upset.

port (PAWRT) *noun* A port is a city or town by the sea where ships can dock.

raw (RAW) *adjective* Raw meat has not been cooked.

rescued (REHS kyood) *verb* Rescued means saved from danger.

risks (RIHSKS) *noun* Risks are the chances people take. They might be hurt by doing something that puts them in danger.

sailors (SAY luhrz) *noun* Sailors are the people who run a ship.

seals (SEELZ) *noun* Seals are animals with smooth skins that live in cold oceans.

stowaway (STOH uh way) *noun* A stowaway is a person who hides on a ship to get a free trip.

stranded (STRAND uhd) *adjective* Stranded means stuck somewhere with no way to leave.

supplies (suh PLYZ) *noun* Supplies are things you need for a job or trip.

survive (suhr VYV) *verb* To survive is to live through a hard time.

thick (THIHK) *adjective* Thick is deep or closely packed.

voyage (VOY ihj) *noun* A voyage is a trip on the ocean.

wreck (REHK) *noun* A wreck is a broken ship.

Index